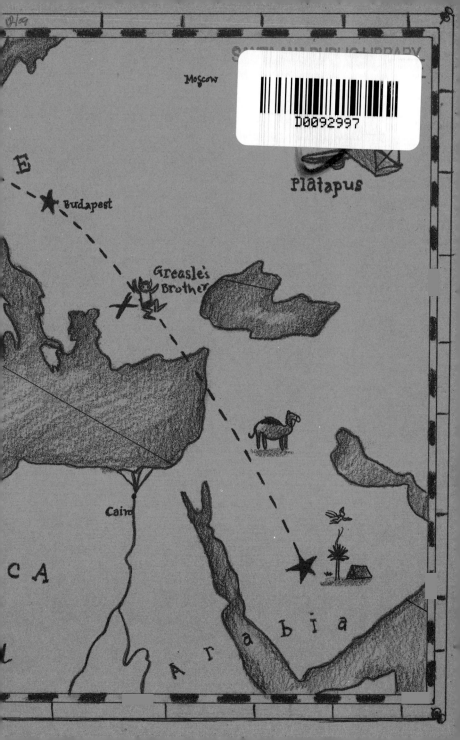

Nathaniel Fludd

Nathaniel Fludd

BEASTOLOGIST

BOOK ONE

FLIGHT OF THE PHOENIX

BY R. L. LaFEVERS

ILLUSTRATED BY KELLY MURPHY

HOUGHTON MIFFLIN BOOKS FOR CHILDREN
Houghton Mifflin Harcourt
BOSTON   NEW YORK   2009

Houghton Mifflin Books for Children is an imprint of
Houghton Mifflin Harcourt Publishing Company.

www.hmhbooks.com

The text of this book is set in ITC Giovanni.
The illustrations are pen and ink.

Library of Congress Cataloging-in-Publication Data is on file.

ISBN 978-0-547-23865-4

Manufactured in the United States of America
MP 10 9 8 7 6 5 4 3 2 1

To Eric,

FOR ALL THOSE HAPPY HOURS

WE SPENT SITTING ON THE FLOOR,

PLAYING THE Animal Game

—R.L.L.

To John,

A BROTHER EXPLORER

—K.M.

Chapter One

*I*T WAS ONE OF THE MOST IMPORTANT MOMENTS in Nathaniel Fludd's young life, and he was stuck sitting in the corner. Miss Lumpton had promised him an overnight trip to the city to visit the zoo. Instead, he found himself in a stuffy office with their suitcases at his feet and his sketchbook in his lap. He'd been given clear instructions not to listen in on Miss Lumpton's conversation with the lawyer. The problem was, they sat only three feet away and the lawyer spoke rather loudly. Nate tried to concentrate on his drawing.

"Thank you for coming on such short notice," the lawyer said.

Nate drummed his heels on one of the suitcases to try to drown out the sound of their voices. Miss Lumpton shushed him.

He stopped kicking.

"You said you had news?" Miss Lumpton asked.

The lawyer lowered his voice, and Nate felt as if his ears grew a bit, straining to hear. "We've had word of his parents." Nate's head jerked up.

Miss Lumpton caught him looking. "Keep drawing," she ordered, then turned back to the lawyer. Nate kept his eyes glued to the sketchbook in front of him. But even though his pencil was moving dutifully on the paper, every molecule of his body was focused on the lawyer's words.

"On May twenty-third of this year, the airship *Italia* crashed on the ice near the North Pole."

Nate's pencil froze. His body felt hot, then cold. He hadn't even known his parents were on an airship.

The lawyer continued. "After months of searching, only eight of the sixteen crew have been found. The boy's parents were not among them."

Miss Lumpton put a hand to her throat. "So what does that mean, exactly?" Her voice wobbled.

"It means that, as of this day, September fifth, 1928, Horatio and Adele Fludd have been declared lost at sea."

"I thought you said they crashed on the ice?" Nate blurted out. Luckily, Miss Lumpton was too busy fishing for her handkerchief to notice he spoke out of turn.

"Yes, well, technically, the ice was frozen seawater," the lawyer said. "But either way, I'm afraid your parents aren't coming back." Miss Lumpton began to cry quietly.

Nate hadn't seen his parents in more than three years. Of course, he'd missed them horribly when they first left. He'd been comforted only when they promised to send for him on his eighth birthday.

"You need a little more time to grow up," his father had said. "When you're old enough to travel well and your sense of adventure has developed, we'll send for you then."

Time had passed. On his eighth birthday, Nate had been excited, but nervous, too. He wasn't sure his love of adventure had shown up yet. But his parents' letter asking him to join them never showed up, either. "Just as well," Miss Lumpton had sniffed. "Their job is much too important to have a youngster tagging along, getting in the way."

On his ninth birthday Nate had been hopeful. Miss Lumpton told him not to be silly. His parents' work was much too dangerous for a young boy. Especially a young boy like himself, one who liked quiet walks, reading, and drawing. Clearly he wasn't suited to a life of adventure. Nate was a little disappointed—he thought he had felt the smallest beginning of an adventurous spark.

By his tenth birthday, Nate had buried the memory of his parents and never took it out anymore. Much like a toy he'd outgrown, he told himself. But the truth was, thinking of them hurt too much.

And now he would never see them again.

Miss Lumpton dabbed at her eyes with the handkerchief. "So the poor boy is all alone in the world?"

Nate wished she'd stop crying. It wasn't *her* parents who'd been lost at sea.

"No, no, my dear Miss Lumpton," the lawyer said. "That is not the case at all. The boy is to live with a Phil A. Fludd."

Miss Lumpton stopped crying. "Phil A. Fludd? Well, who is that, I'd like to know."

The lawyer studied the paper in front of him. "A cousin of the boy's father. Lives in Batting-at-the-Flies up in North County."

Miss Lumpton sniffed. "Well, what about me?"

Suddenly Nate understood why she'd been crying. She hadn't been worried about him at all.

"They've left you a Tidy Sum, Miss Lumpton. You shall not want."

Miss Lumpton's tears disappeared. She sat up straighter and leaned forward. "How much?"

The lawyer told her the amount of money she would receive. Her cheeks grew pink with pleasure. "Well, that should do very nicely."

"In fact," the lawyer said, "my clerk is holding the funds for you. If you'd like to check with him when we're done—"

Miss Lumpton stood up. "I think we're done."

Nate looked at her in surprise. *He* didn't think they were done. He didn't understand why he couldn't stay with Miss Lumpton. Why couldn't things go on the way they had for the past three years?

His governess came over to where he sat and gave him

an awkward pat on the head. "Good luck, dear boy." She grabbed one of the suitcases and left the room in search of her Tidy Sum.

Nate did feel like crying then. Instead, he blinked quite fast.

"Now," the lawyer boomed, "we must go, too." He pulled a pocket watch from his vest and looked at it. "You have a train to catch."

"A train?" Nate asked.

"Yes. Now put that book of yours away and come along." The lawyer closed his watch with a snap. "Eh, what have you drawn there?" he asked. "A walrus?"

"Er, yes." Nate shut the sketchbook quickly, before the lawyer could recognize himself.

"Well, do hurry. It wouldn't do to miss the train. It wouldn't do at all." The lawyer came out from behind his desk and grabbed Nate's suitcase.

Nate stood up and tucked his sketchbook under his arm. The lawyer clamped his hand onto Nate's shoulder and steered him out of the office.

Nate had to take giant steps to keep up. The train station was only two blocks away, but Nate was out of breath by the time they got there.

"All aboard!" the conductor called out.

"Here." The lawyer thrust the suitcase at Nate and shoved a ticket into his hand. "Hurry, boy! They won't hold the train for you." His voice was gruff and impatient. Nate wondered if the lawyer would get a Tidy Sum for getting him on the train.

Once he was onboard, Nate hurried to the window to wave goodbye, but the lawyer had already left.

Chapter Two

THE TRAIN DIDN'T ARRIVE IN BATTING-AT-THE-FLIES until late afternoon. Nate was the only one who got off. An old dog slept in the doorway of the station, a swarm of flies buzzing idly around his head. As Nate walked toward him, the door opened and an old, bent man came out. He studied Nate. "You must be the newest Fludd. C'mon, I'm to give you a ride up to the farm."

The stationmaster tossed Nate's suitcase into the back of a wagon harnessed to an old horse. Then he and Nate climbed in. The stationmaster clicked his tongue, and the horse set off at a slow clop.

They rode through a rolling green countryside dotted with farmhouses and cottages. Sheep stood in the pastures, twitching their tails lazily. Something about their dull, placid faces reminded Nate of Miss Lumpton. His eyes stung and his throat grew tight. He opened his sketchbook, took out his pencil, and began to draw one of the sheep.

He sketched until the wagon turned down a rutted road and a rambling farmhouse came into view. The house was slightly rundown, with rough stone walls and a thatched roof that jutted out at a steep angle, like a bristly mustache. Two monstrous brick chimneys loomed against the skyline. Towers and gables stuck out from all sorts of odd angles.

It looked as though it probably had bats. Nate's heart sank as the wagon rolled to a stop.

"Here ye go, then," the stationmaster said. The old man hopped down and unloaded Nate's suitcase. Before Nate could say thank you, the man tipped his cap, climbed back in, and turned the horse back toward the village.

Nate picked his way up the path, which was overgrown with weeds and brambles. The front door was sturdy and thick and needed a new coat of paint. The brass door knocker was shaped like the head of a snarling lion or a snarling man—Nate couldn't be sure which. He reached gingerly around its sharp teeth and knocked on the door.

Nothing happened.

As he waited, he noticed a brass plaque above the door: P. A. FLUDD, BEASTOLOGIST.

He'd never heard of a beastologist before. That could be

interesting. Except that thinking of beasts had him thinking of bats again. He glanced up at the shadows under the eaves, then lifted the knocker and rapped harder.

Finally, he heard the sound of footsteps from inside the house. The door jerked open as a voice said, "I told you. I don't have anything else for your charity bazaar. Now, do leave me alone—oh. Hello."

Nate took a step back and stared at the person in the doorway. She was tall with lots of elbows and knees and angles poking about, which reminded him of a giraffe. Her hair was pulled back, but little wisps escaped. A giraffe with a mane, Nate corrected. His fingers itched for his pencil. Instead, he drew himself up to his full height like Miss Lumpton used to do. "I am Nathaniel Fludd. Would you please inform the master of the house that I have arrived?"

"Oh-ho! A bit of a nib, are you?" The woman looked amused. "*I* am the master of the house, young Nate. Phil A. Fludd, at your service."

Nate blinked. This was his father's long-lost cousin? "B-but you're a *she*," he said.

"Phil is short for Philomena. The *A* is for Augusta. My parents couldn't decide between Latin and Greek. I'm sure

you can understand why I go by Phil. You may call me Aunt Phil, if you prefer."

Nate was unsure what to do. He couldn't have imagined someone less like Miss Lumpton if he'd tried. A wave of homesickness swept through him, and he fought the urge to run all the way back to the train station.

"You look just like your father, when he was your age," the old woman said.

Her words chased all thoughts of flight out of his head. "I do?"

"Yes, very much so."

"Did you know my father well?" Nate asked shyly.

"Of course I did! I taught him half of what he knows. *Knew*," she corrected. Her voice softened. "I'm very sorry about your parents, Nate." They stood awkwardly for a moment before Aunt Phil cleared her throat. "Well, come in. I'm quite busy and it's nearly dinnertime."

She grabbed his suitcase, picking it up as if it weighed no more than an umbrella. Halfway through the front hall, she turned back toward him. "Well, do come on."

Pushing his homesickness aside, Nate followed her into his new home.

Chapter Three

*T*HE FIRST THING NATE NOTICED were the maps. They covered the walls like wallpaper. There were maps of the world, some bigger than he was, and maps of oceans and continents and places Nate had never heard of. There was even a map of the moon and the stars.

Globes of all shapes and sizes were scattered throughout the hall. They passed a shelf that held strange instruments. Nate recognized a few of them, such as the telescope and the compass, but others were completely unfamiliar.

Aunt Phil set Nate's suitcase down at the foot of dusty-looking stairs. "I'll show you your room after supper. I've got to get back to the kitchen before it boils over."

Indeed—Nate thought he smelled something burning already.

The kitchen was warm and full of bright yellow light. But it was just as jumbled and cluttered as the rest of the house. Crockery was stacked in wobbly-looking towers. Old dishes and pans filled one side of the sink. On the stove, a giant pot bubbled and hissed, cheerfully sending a small stream of something brown over its side. A large, odd-looking statue of some unusual bird sat in the corner. It was nearly three feet tall and sported a tuft of curly feathers high on its rear. A dodo, Nate thought. His fingers itched to draw it.

"Sit down, sit down," Aunt Phil said, hurrying over to the stove.

Nate brushed the crumbs from a chair, then sat.

She set a bowl of stew in front of him and handed him a thick slice of buttered bread. "I'm going to leave you to your supper. I've loads to do before tomorrow morning. I'm so glad you're here. I was worried you might not make it in time."

Nathaniel wanted to ask, *Make it in time for what?* but his mouth was already full.

"Cornelius here will keep you company." And with that, Aunt Phil disappeared out the back door.

Nate looked around the kitchen, wondering when Cornelius would show up.

"Well, with that hair of yours, you certainly *look* like a Fludd."

Nate jumped at the voice, then whipped his head around to see where it had come from. There was nothing there but the statue of the dodo bird. Unless . . . "You're alive?"

"Very much so."

"B-but . . . you're a dodo!"

"And you're a boy. But I don't hold it against you. Well, not much, anyway."

The stew forgotten, Nate stared. "But you're extinct."

"Well, rare, certainly. There are only four of us left, three of us in captivity. Only I don't think of myself as being captive. More of an honored guest."

"And you talk!"

"Yes, well, so do parrots and mynas, and I'm far more

16

intelligent than they are. A better conversationalist, too. Now, eat your dinner before it congeals."

Under the watchful eye of the dodo, Nate returned to his dinner. He was hungry enough that he barely noticed the burned taste. After a few bites, he looked up at the dodo. "What's a beastologist?"

The dodo's feathers puffed up in agitation. "How can you be a Fludd and not know what a beastologist is?"

Nate hunched his shoulders and turned back to his stew. He should have known better than to ask questions. Miss Lumpton always said it was one of his greatest flaws.

"A beastologist," the dodo said with a sigh, "is someone who studies beasts. Not any old beasts, mind you. Only unusual beasts. Like me." He fluffed his feathers and preened a bit.

Nate risked another question. "You mean like lions and elephants and crocodiles?" Those were the most unusual beasts he could think of. And crocodiles, especially, were fun to draw.

Cornelius snorted. "Nothing as ordinary as those. A beastologist studies only the most rare and exotic beasts."

Nate pushed his empty bowl to the side and asked, "Like what?"

"Like dodos. Or basilisks, or griffins, or manticores and the like."

Nate thought back to the one time Miss Lumpton had taken him to the zoo. He didn't remember seeing any of those. "How come I've never heard of any of those before?"

"Because most people think they're just myths, which is much better for all concerned, if you ask me. Now, if you've finished your dinner," the dodo said, "I'll show you to your room."

Nate followed Cornelius out of the kitchen. The bird waddled sharply from side to side. He was not built for speed—or grace—but then, neither was Nate.

When the dodo reached the stairs, he did a little fluttering hop up onto the first step. "Best grab your suitcase," he said.

Nate peered up into the darkness. If there were any bats, they probably lived up there. "Aren't there any bedrooms down here?" he asked.

"Don't be silly." The dodo paused on the second stair. "You're not afraid, are you?"

The scorn in the dodo's voice nudged Nate onto the first stair. "Of course not," he said, then followed Cornelius the rest of the way.

Once upstairs, the dodo led Nate to one of the very last doors in the dark hallway. "Here you go. Open it, why don't you?"

Nate opened the door and stepped into a small, dusty room.

"The water closet's at the north end of the hall," Cornelius explained. "I wouldn't bother unpacking tonight. Until morning, then." The bird left the room and waddled back down the hall to the stairs.

Nate set his suitcase down and tried to get his bearings. The ceiling slanted down toward the wall. A small bed sat tucked up under the eaves. There was a map in here, too, over by the closet. Nate went for a closer look.

It was old, and the words were written in Latin. It appeared to be a map of the world, but it was unlike any Nate had ever seen. For one, the continents were all the wrong shape and size, and there weren't enough oceans. But the most unusual thing about it was that it was covered in pictures. There were men in crowns, whom Nate took to be kings, but other men—strange men—had no heads or only one eye, or instead of walking on two legs appeared to be hopping on only one. And the animals! Nate recognized an elephant and a crocodile, but there were many others he'd never seen before. The map was signed down in the corner with great flourish by a Sir Mungo Fludd. Next to his signature was a blue and gold starburst with a dodo in the middle.

There was a loud clatter and thump from somewhere outside. Nate turned from the map and went to look out the window. He blew aside a small pile of dead flies on the windowsill, then pressed his nose to the cold glass.

Torches were lit down in the yard, where Nate could make out an enormous, strange wing-shaped object. A beast, perhaps? No, it was an airplane, he finally realized.

Why did Aunt Phil have an airplane in her backyard? He pressed closer to the glass and saw Aunt Phil loading supplies into the cargo hold. She was getting ready to go on a trip.

His heart sank. Who was going to watch him? The dodo?

Surely it would have been better for him just to stay in his old house with Miss Lumpton. Except, he reminded himself, Miss Lumpton wanted her Tidy Sum more than him.

Discouraged, he went over and set his suitcase on the bed. Best get this horrible day behind him and get some sleep. He opened the suitcase to collect his pajamas, then stopped.

There was a carefully folded pink flannel nightgown, two pairs of woolen stockings, a stack of old letters, and a pair of women's drawers.

Cheeks flaming with embarrassment, he slammed the lid shut. He'd gotten Miss Lumpton's suitcase by mistake!

Tears, hot and prickly, stung his eyes. He jammed his fists into them and rubbed hard. Feeling miserable, he slipped out of his jacket and shoes and climbed into the strange bed. The sheets felt colder than normal, the blanket thinner. He huddled under the covers and missed his own bed. He missed the bedtime stories Miss Lumpton read to him, even if they were a bit boring.

Unable to sleep, he got up and fetched his sketchbook and pencil. He crawled back under the covers and propped himself up on the pillows. He chewed the end of the pencil, trying to remember what his parents looked like. By the time he fell asleep, all he'd been able to draw was his father's mustache and the small beauty mark on his mother's chin.

Chapter Four

"W<small>AKE UP,</small> N<small>ATE.</small>" A hand gently shook his shoulder. "Time to get up, dear. We must be off."

"What? Huh?" Nate sat up and rubbed his eyes, wondering where he was. When he caught sight of the strange woman leaning over his bed, it all came rushing back to him.

"How clever of you to have slept in your clothes," Aunt Phil said. "You won't even have to get ready this morning."

"I slept in my clothes because I don't have any pajamas. I got Miss Lumpton's suitcase by mistake."

"That's just as well, as we'll have to travel light."

Still trying to clear the sleep from his brain, Nate looked at her in puzzlement.

"Didn't Cornelius tell you?"

"Tell me what?"

"That we had to leave first thing this morning?"

Nate shook his head. He was certain the dodo hadn't mentioned anything of the sort.

"That dodo." Aunt Phil shook her head in exasperation. "Well, we must hurry. I want to take off before the wind picks up."

It finally dawned on Nate. "You mean you want *me* to go with you?"

Aunt Phil's face softened. "But of course. What did you think I'd do? Leave you behind with nothing but old Cornelius for company?"

Nate began fiddling with the edge of the blanket.

"Oh dear. That's exactly what you thought." Aunt Phil sat down on the bed next to him. "I'm not sure why your parents didn't take you with them, Nate, but normally all Fludds begin their training by the time they're eight. By my calculations, you're two years overdue."

Nate stopped fiddling with the blanket. Aunt Phil's words had jogged a memory loose. "They said they'd send for me when I turned eight," he said. "But they never did."

"Surely they explained their reasons to you in their letters?"

Nate's fingers found the blanket corner again. "There weren't any letters."

"What?" Aunt Phil sounded shocked. She stood up and began pacing. "That's not right," she muttered. "They should have sent you letters."

Although he was glad to have her sympathy, Nate felt he should defend his parents. "Maybe they were too busy," he suggested.

"No, no. Fludds always write letters." She stopped pacing and glanced out the window. "There is so much to explain and so little time. It will have to wait until later. We really must take off before that wind picks up."

She took a rucksack from the dresser and tossed it onto the bed. "You can pack your things in there," she said. "Meet me in the kitchen." She turned to leave.

"Wait!" Nate called out.

Aunt Phil paused at the door.

"Where are we going?" Nate asked.

"To Arabia, Nate. We have to oversee the birth of the new phoenix. It happens only once every five hundred years," she said. "So we can't be late!"

A *phoenix!* Nate thought as he stuffed his feet into his shoes. But they were myths. Legends.

Something hot and itchy rose in his chest. He couldn't tell if it was fear or excitement. Cornelius had told him that beastologists dealt with beasts that other people thought were myths. Nate had thought the bird was just trying to make himself seem important.

He shrugged into his jacket sleeves, then grabbed his sketchbook and pencil and shoved them into the rucksack. As he hurried toward the stairs, he hoped he'd get breakfast before they left.

Nate took three wrong turns before he reached the kitchen, but he hardly even noticed. He wasn't going to be left behind this time—he could barely get his mind around that.

As he approached the kitchen, he caught raised voices. "You were supposed to tell him about the phoenix." It was Aunt Phil.

"Yes, well, seeing as he didn't even know what a beast-ologist was, that seemed to be putting the cart before the horse. Are you sure taking him with you is a good idea?" Nate stopped cold at Cornelius's words.

"Of course it is. He's a Fludd and it's long past time he began his training."

"Yes, but there are Fludds and then there are *Fludds*. He is rather lacking in the basic Fludd talents. When I told him the water closet was down the hall to the north, he looked south."

Aunt Phil sniffed loudly. "So he needs a good compass. Nothing wrong with that."

"Except when you are going into dangerous territory and he's your backup."

"He's the only Fludd left besides me—"

"Which is exactly my point. We can't afford to lose any more of you. Perhaps he should stay here with me. We can work on the basics, and then when you return, he won't be so far behind. He'll have some skills for you to work with."

The dodo's words made Nate squirm. Even a stupid, supposed-to-be-extinct bird knew he wasn't a proper Fludd.

Even worse, it sounded as though his lack of skill would put them in danger.

Blindly, Nate turned around to escape back the way he'd come. He'd hide in one of those old rooms till Aunt Phil left, and then he'd find a way to sneak back to his own house. Except when he turned, he went left instead of right and bumped smack into a bureau. A pair of silver candlesticks tumbled to the floor with a clang.

"Nate! Is that you?" Aunt Phil's fuzzy head appeared in the doorway. "Come on in. Your breakfast is getting cold."

Not wanting to admit he'd overheard them, Nate shuffled into the kitchen, careful not to meet Cornelius's eye. "Miss Lumpton says birds are dirty and have mites," he muttered.

The dodo puffed up and opened his beak to say something, but Aunt Phil shushed him.

Once Nate had taken a seat, Aunt Phil plunked a platter of bacon and eggs in front of him. Nate poked at the flat fried egg that was burned around the edges. "I always have a boiled egg for breakfast," he said. He'd long ago learned to stop asking for anything else. "And porridge," he added. "But I think I'm allergic to porridge."

"Well, you're safe. There's no porridge here. Bacon and eggs are all I've got," Aunt Phil said. "I suggest you eat up. It may well be our last hot breakfast for quite a while." She took a seat across from him, but instead of eating her breakfast, she unrolled a large map. "Do you know where Arabia is?" she asked.

"No, ma'am," Nate said around a bite of bacon. "I'm not allowed to look at maps."

"Why ever not?" Aunt Phil asked.

"Miss Lumpton thinks they remind me of my parents."

"Well, rightfully so," Aunt Phil said roundly. "Your parents were mapmakers, after all."

"She thinks talking about them upsets me."

"And does it?" Aunt Phil asked.

Nate shrugged and took another bite of bacon. After a long moment, Aunt Phil turned back to the map. "Well, Arabia is in the Near East. We'll fly across the channel to France, then down across Europe to Turkey. We'll clip the Mediterranean Sea, then land in Arabia. We'll stop for a short rest and refueling near Budapest."

Almost against his will, Nate's eyes went to the top of the map. The North Pole.

Aunt Phil saw where he was looking. She put her finger just above a tiny speck of land. "That's where the airship went down. Spitsbergen."

Nate's throat grew thick and tight. He cleared it and pointed to the familiar gold and blue starburst down in the bottom left-hand corner. "What's that?" It had been on all the maps Nate had seen so far.

"A compass rose," Aunt Phil explained. "The Fludd compass rose, to be exact. It's how you can tell if a map was drawn by a Fludd or someone else. Now, it's time to go. Got your rucksack?"

"Yes, ma'am. Right here." He patted his lap.

"Excellent. Here. You'll need a few more things." She handed him a canteen, a close-fitting leather cap, a muffler, and a pair of funny-looking round glasses encased in leather. "Goggles. To keep the bugs and dust out," she explained.

Feeling a little more prepared, Nate followed Aunt Phil to the door.

"We'll see you in a week or two, Cornelius."

The old dodo glanced at Nate. "Hopefully," he drawled.

Nate turned to the dodo. *Mites,* he silently mouthed.

Cornelius squawked and puffed up his feathers. Aunt Phil grabbed Nate's elbow and dragged him outside.

Up close, in broad daylight, the plane looked old and rickety—flimsy, even. The fabric skin was ripped and patched in places. The metal covering the front was dented and pitted. "Will this thing really fly?" Nate asked.

"Of course it will," Aunt Phil said, steering him to the nose of the plane. "This Sopwith Platypus performed spectacularly in the Great War and still has a lot of good years left in it."

"Why is it called a platypus?" he asked.

"Because it's comfortable landing on both water and land. Now stop dawdling and get up on that barrel. When I give the signal, grab hold of the propeller and give a hard yank."

Aunt Phil left to go climb into the plane. Steadying the barrel with both hands, Nate clambered up onto it, hoping the whole thing wouldn't tip over. Slowly, he stood up. When the engine sputtered to life, his whole body rumbled with the force of it.

"Now!" she shouted.

Stretching up on his tiptoes, Nate grasped the propeller blade with both hands and pulled down hard.

His hands slid off the prop as if they'd been greased. He stared down at them, dumbfounded.

"Probably oil from the barrel," Aunt Phil shouted at him over the engine noise. "Here." She tossed him a rag. He reached out and caught it, surprising himself.

"Good catch! Wipe your hands before you try again."

Nate did as he was told, then stuffed the rag into his pocket.

"Ready?" Aunt Phil yelled.

"Ready!" he yelled back.

"Now!"

This time when he pulled down on the propeller, it spun, slowly at first and then faster and faster. Afraid he'd be chopped into bits, Nate leaped down off the barrel, causing it to tip over. A thick, heavy liquid began to *glug-glug* all over the grass.

"Careful, Nate, that's worth a pretty penny!" Aunt Phil called out.

Nate quickly righted the barrel, wiped his hands on the rag again, then hurried over and climbed into the tiny, cramped cockpit. He busied himself fastening his helmet and positioning the goggles over his eyes.

"Hold on," Aunt Phil cried, and the airplane lurched forward. The roar of the engine drowned out everything else. Nate gripped the sides as the plane rolled and bumped its way across the field. When it picked up speed, his stomach fluttered and he couldn't tell if he was going to giggle or throw up.

As they hurtled down the field, Nate realized they were running out of room. The neighbor's house was coming up in front of them. Fast.

The engine continued to roar, the motor straining with the effort. The house drew closer. Just as Nate was about to duck, the motor gave a final whine and the plane lurched upward. As the ground fell away, Nate's stomach felt as if it dropped down to his toes.

He wasn't sure, but he thought one of the wheels clipped the chimney as they flew by.

Chapter Five

NATE WAS TORN BETWEEN EXCITEMENT AND TERROR as they climbed higher and higher into the air. The breakfast he'd eaten earlier felt like lead rocks in his stomach. Below him, the entire world fell away, growing smaller and smaller until it looked like one of the maps on Aunt Phil's walls.

Once he realized the plane would stay in the air and not go crashing to the ground, he had to admit it was thrilling to soar through the sky like a bird. Without warning, they plowed into a fluffy white cloud. Nate gasped at the shock-

ing, damp cold of it. Just as quickly, they emerged once again into the early morning sun.

They passed a small flock of geese flying in formation. Nate wasn't sure who was more surprised, him or the geese. Nate quickly noticed that the higher they climbed, the colder it got. He was glad of his helmet and jacket and wished he had a pair of gloves. His hands were white and numb with cold.

Or maybe he was just hanging on too tightly. He relaxed his grip, his fingers tingling as the blood flow returned.

When they'd been in the air for more than an hour, the excitement of his first flight wore off. The airplane was loud and stank of petrol. It vibrated so hard that Nate was certain it would shake his teeth loose. He was cold and cramped, and there was nothing to do but count the stitches on Aunt Phil's leather helmet in front of him.

Nate quickly became drowsy. He remembered reading somewhere that people fell asleep just before they died of exposure, so he tried to fight it. In the end, he decided if he had to freeze to death, it would be better to be asleep than awake.

Nate awoke with a start as the plane touched down in the night. They bounced along a bumpy road lit by a searchlight mounted on the front of the plane. As his eyes adjusted to the dark, Nate also saw torches lining the runway.

After another minute of bouncing, the plane shuddered to a stop. Nate checked his limbs to be sure he was all in one piece.

"Well, we've arrived in Budapest. Do you want to stretch your legs?" Aunt Phil asked.

Nate very much did want to stretch his legs. Without wasting another second, he scrambled out of the plane and joined Aunt Phil on the ground. A group of men stood before a small fire in front of a rough-looking shack.

Aunt Phil cupped her hand around her mouth. "Halloo! We're here to refuel."

The men nodded and began talking among themselves in a strange language. Two hurried into the shack, then came back out carrying a ladder and a huge funnel. The others had already reached the plane and began unloading fuel cans from the cargo hold.

"They seem to know just what to do," Nate said.

"Of course they do. They refuel the airmail service that runs from London to Budapest. They're old hands at this."

Nate watched as a man climbed up the ladder and began pouring the fuel into the airplane's fuselage through the large funnel. The smell of petrol filled the air.

"I'm going to catch a quick wink while they fill the plane," Aunt Phil said. "They've plenty of cots in there, so you're welcome to do the same. Or wander around and explore a bit, whatever you'd prefer." With that, Aunt Phil disappeared into the shack.

The first thing Nate did was go find some privacy behind the nearby bushes. When he returned, three of the men were still refueling the plane, but the rest had returned to their fire. He wasn't sure what to do, so he wandered over toward them, feeling shy. They stopped talking when he drew close. One of them pointed to his hair, then nudged the man next to him. The other man nodded and smiled. "*Flutt,*" he said, and they all laughed. But it was a friendly laugh, so Nate smiled back.

Someone shoved a bowl of hot stew into his hand. *Goulash,* they called it. As Nate wolfed it down, one of the men took out a flutelike instrument and began to play softly.

When Nate was done, he thanked the men and went inside the shack. He was surprised at how tired he was, since he'd slept most of the flight over. He fumbled around until he found an empty cot. He settled under the blanket, warm and full with the strange music sounding softly in his ears. Maybe travel wouldn't be that bad after all.

The next morning, they were back in the plane and on their way before the sun had risen. Things quickly returned to the bone-rattling monotony of the day before. Nate hunched down to stay as warm as possible.

Some time later, Aunt Phil twisted around in her seat. "Something's wrong with the propeller," she called back to him. "I think some debris has gotten tangled up in it. We need to remove whatever it is before the prop stops altogether."

Nate's chest suddenly felt hollow.

"Feel like stretching your legs?" she yelled.

Before Nate could ask what that had to do with the propeller, she shoved a piece of rope at him. "Here. Slip this around your waist."

Wrenching around in the cramped seat, Nate did as he was told.

"There," Aunt Phil yelled when he had it secure. "Now take these and you're all set." She thrust a pair of leather gloves at him. She kept talking as he tugged them on. "I'll slow her down so you can climb out onto the wing and make your way to the propeller. But if I have to slow down too much, we'll stall. So be quick."

Nate looked at her in disbelief. Surely she didn't mean for him to—

"Hurry, Nate! I don't want the prop to give up altogether! Then we'll stall for sure."

Did she mean for him to crawl out onto the nose of the plane to fix the problem? He felt a sharp yank at the rope around his waist. "Get moving!"

Apparently, she did. Very glad for the rope that anchored him to the plane, Nate stood up. Struggling to keep his balance, he crawled out of the cockpit and lowered his feet over the side until they touched the wing. Gripping the side of the plane for dear life, he shuffled his feet along the wing, inching closer to the propeller. The plane bucked and dipped, adjusting to his shifting weight. Even with the slower speed, the wind screamed past him, tugging at his shirt, his helmet, his body, trying to dislodge him from his wobbly perch. His heart hammering in his chest, Nate kept his eyes glued to the nose of the plane and tried not to think about how far down the ground was.

His body hugged the side of the plane as he scooched his way forward. When he passed Aunt Phil in her cockpit, she gave him a cheerful thumbs-up sign.

All too soon, he ran out of wing. He shifted his grip to the struts that held the wing to the plane. Searching for a

foothold among the wires and fastenings, he pushed himself atop the nose of the plane.

He sat there for a moment, trying to catch his breath. He tried to peer down into the propeller but had to jerk his nose back to keep it from being whacked off by the blades. They were moving so fast, he couldn't see a thing.

Clinging to the searchlight mount, he put his hand down to where the propeller met the nose of the plane. He groped cautiously, feeling for something that might be causing the problem.

There was a sharp pinch as his glove got caught in the propeller gear. Alarmed, he yanked his hand back. As he did, something flew out from behind the propeller into midair. It happened so fast, Nate wasn't able to get a good look at it before it disappeared far below.

But the propeller stopped lagging. Nate realized he had somehow managed to fix the problem. Before he could congratulate himself, there was a flurry of movement. With a howl, a small shape launched itself from the propeller toward Nate's face.

Chapter Six

THE CREATURE—A BAT?—LATCHED ON TO NATE and began pounding and scratching at his head. Nate tucked his chin under and tried to protect his face. Gripping the nose of the plane hard with both knees, he let go with one hand and plucked the thing from his head. It dangled in front of his face, swiping and kicking.

What was it?

It was about the size of a kitten but sort of human shaped. It was covered with engine oil and gear grease. Large pointed ears stuck out from black hair. It was hard to tell, but Nate thought it might be a girl thing . . . whatever it was. After a second, Nate realized the squeaking sounds it was making were actually words.

"That was me brother, you big oaf! What'd you go and do that for?"

The plane dipped, and Nate flattened himself to keep from losing his balance. He had to get back to the cockpit. Fast. But what to do with the creature? Should he just toss it overboard? That might not be such a good idea. Aunt Phil was a beastologist, after all. What if he'd just caught his first beast?

Heartened by this thought—and the fact that it wasn't a bat—Nate began scooting backwards, inch by terrifying inch. In one hand, he kept the small creature out in front of him, well clear of its flying feet and fists. The other hand clutched desperately to the struts as his feet poked around, looking for the firm surface of the wing. When his feet finally connected, he let out a long, shaky breath, then began the slow, terrifying process of making his way back.

He was drenched in sweat by the time he got back to the cockpit and tumbled clumsily into his seat.

"Hey! Watch what yer doing there, you big dolt."

"Oops. Sorry." Nate pulled the creature out from under him.

"Good job, Nate!" Aunt Phil's voice came through the wind noise. "You fixed it."

Nate leaned forward and held the creature aloft. "Look what I found up there. There were two of them, but one fell before I could catch it."

Aunt Phil wrinkled her face in distaste. "Gremlins. Nasty things. Always trying to muck up my plane. You can just toss it over the side. They're pests, really."

Nate looked down into the scrunched-up, ugly little face. Throw it overboard?

The gremlin put her hands together. "Please don't toss me over. Please. I'll be good. I promise. I won't drink any fuel or play with the prop again. Just don't throw me over. Without me brother, I'm all alone in the world." Her eyes grew big and wide as she glanced over the side of the plane.

Nate felt a sharp pang of guilt. He knew all about being alone in the world. He had no idea what would happen to him if Aunt Phil hadn't taken him in. "I'm sorry about your brother," he said. "I didn't mean to kill him."

"Oh, he won't die. He'll land just fine. That's why we got

such big feet, see?" She held hers up for him to inspect. They were large—like rabbits' feet. "He'll just have to find himself another plane. That's all." She sniffed.

Nate turned back to Aunt Phil. "Do I have to throw her over? Can't I just keep her until we land, then let her go?"

Aunt Phil shrugged. "I'm telling you, they're nothing but pests. But if you want, you can shove it into your rucksack until we land. I'll deal with it then."

Nate turned back to the gremlin. "Did you hear that? It's into the rucksack if you want to stay."

The gremlin nodded, then stuck out her tiny hand.

Nate hesitated, then put his finger out, hoping she wouldn't bite it.

She shook his finger solemnly. "Greasle's me name. My brother back there was Oiliver."

"And I'm Nate. Again, I'm sorry about your brother." With his free hand, he opened the rucksack at his feet. "In you go," he said.

Greasle sent him a cheerful wave before she disappeared into the pack.

Hours later, Aunt Phil swiveled around in her seat again. "There it is!"

"There's what?" he yelled back.

"Where we're going."

Nate felt the plane shift directions and begin its descent. He peered down to the ground below. Far, far below. He could see nothing but sand everywhere he looked.

Aunt Phil brought the plane lower. He could make out a ribbon of road that was a little darker than the sand. At one end was a cluster of tents and a few squat buildings.

"Hang on!" Aunt Phil yelled. Nate clutched the sides of the plane and shut his eyes, then jerked them open again. Better to see, he decided.

He could make out people now. Two men in white robes and turbans were waving small flags at Aunt Phil. She shifted the plane a bit to the left, then dropped the nose.

Nate felt dizzy and sick as the ground rushed up. When the plane landed with a bone-jarring thud, his head snapped back and he bit his tongue. The coppery taste of blood filled his mouth.

The whole plane shuddered, and a fountain of sand flew up behind them. Aunt Phil cut the motor and they bounced and jiggled their way to a stop. "That's why they call it a platypus," she said. "A regular plane could never have landed in the sand that easily. Welcome to Arabia, Nate."

That was easy? Nate thought.

The tents that had looked small from the air were actually quite large and sat next to a pen holding a dozen camels. A group of men in billowing white robes and head cloths rushed over to greet them. One of them set a step stool by the plane so Aunt Phil could climb out. When she was down, she motioned to Nate. He grabbed his pack and scrambled over the edge.

The leader folded his hands and gave a small bow. "Greetings, Dr. Fludd. We have everything ready for you, as you requested."

"Thank you, Hakim." Then she began talking to him in an unfamiliar language. Arabian, Nate guessed, since they were in Arabia. When she was done talking, she clamped her hand on to Nate's shoulder and steered him to one of the tents. "We're going to catch a bit of sleep in here until the sun goes down. Then the real adventure will begin," she said with a wink.

Nate gawped at her. He'd had quite enough adventure already, thank you. He wasn't sure he'd survive any more.

Chapter Seven

W*HEN NATE AWOKE*, he found Greasle sitting on his chest, staring at him. Startled, he sat up suddenly and she tumbled to the ground.

"Ow. What'd you go and do that for?" she asked, rubbing her caboose.

"Didn't mean to," Nate muttered. He swung his legs off the cot and rubbed the sand from his eyes. It was cooler than before, he noticed. And darker. He looked around for Aunt Phil.

"She's out talking to those men," Greasle told him. "You got any food on you? 'Cause there was nothing in that pack of yours."

Nate pointed to a platter on a table. She studied it for a moment, then snagged a small brown fruit and took a nibble. She made a face. "I shouldn't have left the plane."

"But that was the agreement," Nate said. "You have to stay in the pack. Actually," he said thoughtfully, "Aunt Phil said she'd deal with you once we landed."

"No!" Greasle squeaked. "I'll be good." She clambered up Nate's leg to his knee and began plucking at his sleeve. "I'll stay in the pack, nice and quiet-like."

"What do you think she'd do to you?" he asked.

Greasle shrugged. "Don't know. Never been caught before."

"Well, just stay quiet in the pack and we'll see what happens. Sometimes grownups forget stuff they've said."

The little gremlin nodded and scampered into the rucksack. Nate hauled it over his shoulder and went to find Aunt Phil.

She was outside, arguing with someone. They were standing in front of two camels piled high with supplies. As Nate approached, the man spoke rapidly, shook his head, then stormed away.

"Is something wrong?" Nate asked.

"There you are. Had a good nap, did you?" Aunt Phil ignored his question.

"Er, yes. What did that man want?"

She sighed. "He was supposed to come with us as a guide, but he backed out. It seems some Bedouin have been sighted in the area and he doesn't want to risk it."

"What are Bedouin?"

"Nomads. They can be a bit territorial."

It sounded to Nate as if the guide was being smart. "Maybe he's right? Maybe it isn't worth the risk?"

"Nonsense. We'll be fine."

"But what will we do for a guide?"

"Why, I'll guide us, of course." Aunt Phil patted one of the large leather bags hanging from one of the camels' saddles. "I've got a Fludd family map and my compass. We'll be fine. Now climb aboard," she said. "The sun is setting and it's cool enough to get started. We'll travel most of the night and sleep during the heat of the day." Aunt Phil cupped her hands for Nate to step into.

He looked from her hands up to the saddle high on top of the camel. "We really have to ride those?"

"Absolutely. These ships of the desert are much heartier for traveling under these conditions. They can go for five whole days without water in the heat of summer, fifty days in winter. Now, do hurry up, Nate. We've a long journey ahead of us and a schedule to keep."

Nate bit back a sigh, clutched a leather strap hanging from the saddle, and placed his foot into Aunt Phil's hands. With a mighty heave, she sent him flying up. He grabbed hold of the saddle horn and scrambled into the saddle.

Aunt Phil gave a firm nod, then went over to mount her camel from a stool.

As Nate sat waiting, his camel turned his long neck around to stare at him. The camel had big liquid brown eyes with long lashes. He was chewing something, his lips working up and down and all around. He did not look happy to have someone on his back. "Nice camel," Nate said, patting the creature's dusty, hairy neck. "Good camel."

The camel gave one last chew, then opened his lips and spit a thick stream of camel saliva at Nate. Nate stared in disgust at the nasty glob plastered to his chest.

"His name is Shabiib," Aunt Phil said from atop her own camel. "You need to show him who's boss." She grabbed her reins and slapped them against her camel's back. "*Hut hut hut!*" she cried. Her camel launched into a fast trot.

Nate grabbed his reins and slapped them like Aunt Phil had done. "*Hut hut hut!*" he cried.

Shabiib turned back around to stare at him, his mobile lips working again. "Don't even think about it!" Nate said. "*Hut hut hut!*" he cried again, this time kicking his heels against the camel's flanks.

Still nothing. He glanced at Aunt Phil, who was far ahead now. Suddenly, there was a loud *thwack* as one of the men gave Shabiib a swat.

The camel launched forward. Nate's teeth crashed together as he slapped down on the camel's back. From inside the pack, Greasle squealed. And if he hadn't been so busy trying to stay on top of the camel, Nate would have checked on her. As it was, all he could do was hang on tightly while excitement and nerves warred in his belly. This was, after all, his last chance to prove he was up to the task of being a Fludd. He had failed his parents. He couldn't risk failing Aunt Phil.

Chapter Eight

*N*ATE STRUGGLED WITH *SHABIIB* as the village quickly disappeared from sight and the last orange rays of the sun shimmered over the endless ocean of sand. It took him a while to learn to relax his body into the rhythm of the camel's stride. The stars had come out by the time Nate finally mastered it. With this small success under his belt, he grew a bit bold. "Aunt Phil?"

"Yes, Nate?"

"You said you'd explain about my parents' writing letters," he reminded her.

Frances Fludd

Henricus Fludd

Octavius
Fludd

Norbert Fludd

Crespi
Fludd

Sir Mungo Fludd

Gaspar Fludd

Mauro Fludd

Isidore Fludd

"Of course." She fell quiet a moment before asking, "What do you know about Fludd family history?"

Nate shrugged. "Not much. Only that Fludds have always been explorers and adventurers." And he was very much *not* an adventurer, he thought but didn't say out loud.

"The first Fludd of record, a Sir Mungo Fludd, became obsessed with Marco Polo's account of his travels to the Orient," Aunt Phil began. "He decided to retrace the journey for himself, only this time with surveyors and cartographers so they could produce a map of the world."

Nate recalled the map on the wall in his room. It had been signed by Sir Mungo Fludd.

"After many years of exploration, he returned and completed the map. He called it *The Geographica, A Map of the World*. However, he knew that he'd seen only a small portion of what the world had to offer. So Sir Mungo had eight sons, one for each cardinal and ordinal point on the compass. When they were grown, he sent them all off in eight different directions. They had orders to explore and survey the world, then report back to him so they could update *The Geographica*. Thus the Age of Exploration had begun.

"After many years, Sir Mungo's seven sons returned, and he compiled the most complete map of all time."

"But what happened to the eighth Fludd? You said there were eight brothers."

Nicholas
Fludd

Flavius
Fludd

Honorius
Fludd

Aunt Phil's face grew dark. "We don't speak of him. Every family has its black sheep, and he's ours."

Nate wanted to ask more about him, but Aunt Phil started talking again.

"Of course, the Fludds saw other things on their travels. New races of man. Strange plants never seen before, and all manner of fearsome beasts. Flavius Fludd, Sir Mungo's great-grandson, began studying these beasts and recorded all his knowledge in *The Book of Beasts*."

"For beastologists?"

"Ah, but there weren't any beastologists yet, Nate." Her face grew troubled. "Now that all sorts of explorers were traveling to these exotic places, they too had discovered the beasts. But being idiots, they hunted and captured the rare creatures until soon there were very few left. After we Fludds discovered the disaster with the dodos, Honorius Fludd declared that from then on, one Fludd in every generation had to dedicate him- or herself to protecting and caring for these beasts. That's when the science of beastology was born."

Nate was quiet for a moment as he absorbed all this. Then he cleared his throat. "But what does that have to do with my parents' letters?" he asked in a very small voice.

Aunt Phil laughed. "Sorry. That was rather the long way about. My point was, for centuries, Fludds have traveled. And for centuries, we have recorded our travels in letters so as to report to those back home. Being an explorer is dangerous work, and we've always known that some of us won't return. Not wanting all our work to be lost, we write letters to record our findings. It's as much a part of being a Fludd as a love of exploration. That's why I'm so sure your parents wrote you letters. You're certain you didn't receive any?"

Nate thought hard, as far back as he could remember. Finally, he shook his head. "No. Only Miss Lumpton got letters. And only once a month."

"Hmmm," Aunt Phil said with a funny look in her eyes. She shook her head, as if clearing it, then changed the subject. "Nate, would you fish my compass out of my saddlebag there? I want to be sure we're on the right course."

Once the sun rose, it didn't take long for the day to heat up. Luckily, they reached the oasis shortly after dawn. There were a number of date palms and a small pool of water surrounded by rocks. Both camels completely ignored the commands to halt and marched straight over to the water. They lowered their heads and began drinking greedily.

"I suppose they've earned it," Aunt Phil said. She reached down and patted her camel on the neck. Nate did the same, but Shabiib stopped drinking and turned around to give him a baleful stare. Afraid the camel would spit at him again, Nate stopped patting.

"Suit yourself," he mumbled.

His rucksack, looped over his saddle horn, began twitching as Greasle wriggled out. "Are we back at the plane yet?" Her small face fell as she looked around the oasis. "What's this place, then?"

"Shh!" Nate hissed, looking around to see if Aunt Phil had heard. Luckily, her camel had finished drinking so she had steered it away from the spring.

Afraid of being left behind, Nate tugged on the reins, trying to get Shabiib to follow. The camel wouldn't budge. Nate tried applying his heels to the camel's flanks. Still nothing.

"Come ON!" Nate said with one final tug at the reins.

Like a shot, Shabiib loped away from the water's edge and galloped after Aunt Phil. Greasle squeaked and Nate tried to pull back on the reins. Then, just as suddenly, Shabiib stopped. Nate found himself airborne, tumbling end over teakettle to land flat on his back in the sand. All the air whooshed out of his lungs. With a final squeal, Greasle landed a few paces to his left.

Shabiib snorted and shook his head, then strolled over to Aunt Phil. Nate struggled to find his breath. "I think I hate camels," he wheezed.

"I told you airplanes were better," said Greasle.

Chapter Nine

"*W*HAT," AUNT PHIL ASKED, "is *that* doing here?"

Nate raised his head from the sand and followed her gaze to Greasle. *Oops.* "She," he corrected without thinking.

Aunt Phil arched an eyebrow at him. "Even so, that doesn't explain why she's here."

Nate got to his feet. "You said I didn't have to throw her overboard," he explained.

"Yes, but I didn't say she could come with us."

"I'm sorry. I thought you didn't want to leave her with the plane."

"I don't!"

"Besides," Nate said, "she's a beast, and you're a beast-ologist. I would think you'd like having her around."

Aunt Phil sniffed. "She's not a true beast. She's just a pest."

Kind of like me, Nate thought. If he couldn't prove himself a true Fludd, he was just a pest dumped on Aunt Phil's doorstep.

Aunt Phil stared at him for a long moment, then threw up her hands and shook her head. "Very well. Keep her. Now let's quit talking and get these camels unloaded." As she turned and strode away, Nate risked a glance at Greasle.

"Phew," she said. "That was close."

"Yes, it was," Nate said. "Now, be good and stay out of trouble."

The gremlin saluted. "Aye, aye, cap'n."

Nate shook his head, then hurried to help Aunt Phil.

Greasle proved to be quite a help in getting the tent set up. Her tiny fingers were especially good at untangling knots. But when Nate pointed that out to Aunt Phil, she merely grunted and shoved a bundle of fragrant sticks at him. "Put those in the tent." He sneezed, then did as instructed.

When the camp was finally set up to Aunt Phil's liking, they settled down to dinner in the tent. Aunt Phil handed Nate a piece of dried goat meat that tasted like salty leather. He tried to hand it back to her.

She shook her head. "Eat it. You'll need to keep up your strength out here."

He choked it down as fast as he could, then popped a date into his mouth. It was sticky and sweet, almost like a piece of toffee. When Aunt Phil wasn't looking, Nate slipped Greasle two dates, then shooed her away to hide behind his rucksack. He wasn't sure how Aunt Phil would feel about sharing food with the gremlin.

Almost as if reading his mind, Aunt Phil looked up. "Where is that pest of yours?" she asked, glancing around the tent.

"Oh, she's already asleep in my rucksack," Nate said. Wanting desperately to change the subject, he asked, "What exactly are we going to do with the phoenix?"

"Well, let's check, shall we?" Aunt Phil turned to one of

her saddlebags. She pulled from it a large, very old-looking book and held it up for Nate to see. *"The Book of Beasts,"* she announced. "The only copy in existence, and so sacred to us Fludds that I would protect the book with my life."

Nate hoped it wouldn't come to that. "Do you have a copy of *The Geographica,* too?"

"No." Aunt Phil's face grew sad. "Your father had the only surviving copy of that book. I'm afraid it was lost at sea with him." They were both silent for a moment, and then Aunt Phil began to read from the book.

> "As the sun sets on the phoenix's five hundredth birthday, it returns to its place of birth and builds a funeral pyre. Amid the rays of the setting sun, it sets itself on fire, burning until it is reduced to a pile of ash.
>
> The secret to a phoenix hatching is to be sure the pile of ash never grows cold."

"How do we do that?" Nate asked.
Aunt Phil continued reading:

> "The nest must be protected from the wind. It is also wise to feed additional fuel to the glowing ash, especially during the cold desert nights."

Aunt Phil stopped reading and looked at Nate.

"Is that it?"

"That's it."

"Well," he said with a smile, "that doesn't sound too hard."

"Of course not," Aunt Phil agreed. "I told you there was nothing to worry about. Good night, Nate."

Aunt Phil snuggled down and was asleep within moments. But when Nate lay down, his mind kept churning through the events of the past three days. Plus, it was too light out to go to sleep. Which gave Nate an idea.

Moving quietly so as not to wake Aunt Phil, he pulled his rucksack closer. He reached inside and got out his sketchbook. Glancing over his shoulder, he angled the paper away from Aunt Phil and began to draw. As his pencil flew across the page, his mind began to sort through all that had happened.

He decided he liked Aunt Phil. Except for her unreasonable dislike of gremlins, she was very nice. Even better, she told him stuff. Important stuff that no other grownup had ever taken the time to tell him before. She also didn't leave him behind, no matter how lacking he was in Fludd skills.

"Whatcha doin'?"

Nate jerked in surprise at Greasle's voice next to his ear. "Drawing," he whispered, closing the book.

"I wanna see," Greasle said.

"Shh! You'll wake Aunt Phil."

Greasle tugged on the book. "But I wanna see," she whined.

"Oh, all right." Nate opened to the page on which he'd been drawing. Greasle pointed to the picture he'd drawn of her. "What's that?"

"You," he said.

She tilted her head and studied the page. "Is that what I look like?"

He glanced down at the drawing. "Yep."

"Pretty, aren't I?"

Nate looked at her

big, round eyes, her batlike ears, and her sharp little teeth. "Quite pretty," he said, trying not to smile.

"And what's that?" she asked, pointing to the facing page.

"A map," Nate whispered, closing the book. He didn't want Aunt Phil to know he'd tried his hand at mapmaking. He wasn't very good at it.

"It's not as pretty as the picture of me," Greasle pointed out.

"No, it's not," Nate agreed. He put the sketchbook aside. "Now let's get some sleep."

Nate was awakened by the most beautiful music he had ever heard. The notes were pure and lovely, but haunting as well, as if sadness might be just around the corner. He pushed to his knees. Greasle was already at the tent opening, peeking out. He joined her. "What is that?"

She wiped an oily tear from her eye. "Don't know."

Nate stepped outside and saw Aunt Phil standing nearby. The music grew louder and she pointed to the horizon.

Nate could make out a bright shape against the darkening sky.

"The phoenix!" he whispered.

"The phoenix," Aunt Phil agreed. "Shh, now. We don't want to startle it."

Nate stood transfixed as the brilliant red and gold bird approached. The phoenix swooped into the oasis area, its tail feathers streaming behind like an orange comet. Sweet, soaring music filled the air as the phoenix circled overhead once, before landing on a palm tree.

As the last of the setting sun's golden rays spread across the desert, the phoenix gave a final burst of song, then erupted into flames.

Nate gasped in surprise. Greasle squeaked and dived under the nearest bedroll. Nate watched the pillar of fire in stunned silence. He hadn't truly believed Aunt Phil. Not really. Not until this minute. But there really *were* magical beasts in this world. And he really would get to help take care of one. This was turning out much better than he had imagined!

As they continued to watch, the flames crackled yellow,

then orange, then red. There was a flash of green flame just before the fire died out.

Now that the fire was silent, Nate heard a noise—a low rumbling sound. Almost like thunder. He looked up to the ridge above the oasis, and fear punched him in the belly.

Outlined against the dusky sky, a score of men riding camels galloped toward them, their curved swords drawn. Afraid, Nate quickly slipped back into the tent and hoped they hadn't seen him.

Chapter Ten

"*The Bedouin,*" *Nate heard Aunt Phil whisper.* Peeking out through the tent flap, he watched them approach. The leader halted his camel and dismounted, then strode toward Aunt Phil.

He studied her suspiciously. "Are you a Turk?"

"No," Aunt Phil replied. "I am a Fludd. Perhaps you've heard of us?"

The leader shook his head. "No Fludds here. You are trespassing and must leave."

"You speak English?" Aunt Phil sounded surprised.

"We fought with British soldiers against the Turks. In the Great War, many years ago."

"Ah, I see. Well, there is no war now, and I am just a scientific observer," she said.

"You are still trespassing," the leader repeated. "This oasis belongs to us." Anger flashed in his eyes. "You must leave."

Aunt Phil shook her head. "I'm very sorry, but I can't leave until I've done what I came for."

"Are you refusing?" He sounded as if he couldn't quite believe it. Nate couldn't either.

"Yes. I really must insist that I stay. But it will be only for a short while."

Instead of answering, the Bedouin leader shouted out instructions to his men. They began to descend upon Aunt Phil. She took one look at the advancing men, then turned back to their leader. "Very well, then. I ask that you grant me hospitality."

A murmur of surprise rose up from the group. The leader narrowed his eyes and gave Aunt Phil an assessing look. "You know of Bedouin hospitality?"

Aunt Phil nodded. "I know if anyone, friend or enemy,

asks for Bedouin hospitality, you are honor bound to grant them food, water, and shelter for three days."

The Bedouin leader did not look happy that she knew this. He looked around the oasis. "You are alone?"

Aunt Phil hesitated but a second before nodding. "Yes, I am alone."

"Very well. Our code of honor demands we grant you hospitality. But only for three days. After that, you will experience Bedouin justice for your crime of trespassing." His voice was harsh, and Nate wondered what exactly Bedouin justice would be.

They waited while Aunt Phil mounted her camel, and then they led her camel and Shabiib from the oasis. At the ridge, Aunt Phil paused and looked back over her shoulder.

Nate stood just inside the tent, watching helplessly as the only person who cared anything about him was taken away.

Chapter Eleven

GREASLE TURNED TO LOOK AT NATE, her eyes wide. "Now what?"

Nate could only stare at the empty space where Aunt Phil had just been. "I don't know." He felt numb and hollow inside. How was he supposed to survive without her? Let alone accomplish their mission with the phoenix? This was a disaster. Cornelius was right: Nate wasn't cut out to be a Fludd. A true Fludd would know what to do, and Nate hadn't the faintest idea.

"Maybe we should follow her," he finally suggested. He took a step forward to leave the shelter of the tent. Greasle pinched him.

"Ouch!"

"Not so fast. Look."

He peered past the tent flap to where the gremlin pointed. A lone sentry stood up on the ridge, watching the Bedouin depart. If Nate tried to follow, he'd be spotted and captured, too.

He slipped back inside the tent and sat down—hard—to try to think. They had enough food and water for five days. With Aunt Phil gone, the supplies would last him and Greasle even longer. Besides, Aunt Phil had gone to great lengths to keep his presence hidden. Clearly, she meant for him to stay here and watch over the phoenix's ashes while she . . . *what?*

Nate's mind slammed into a wall when he tried to guess what might happen to her.

"I wouldn't worry too much about that old witch," Greasle said, scrunching up her face. "She knows how to take care of herself. The mean ones usually do."

Nate looked in surprise at the gremlin.

"What?" she said. "She's not nice to us gremlins. Not like you are." Greasle reached out and gave Nate's arm a shy little pet.

This heartened Nate somewhat. He seemed to be doing a good job with Greasle, even if Aunt Phil didn't consider her a true beast. Maybe that meant there was a chance he could help the phoenix. He'd never know until he tried.

"I guess it's up to us." He scooped Greasle up onto his shoulder, went to the tent flap, and peeked outside. The sentry was gone. Safely alone now, Nate crossed the sand to the palm tree.

"What if she doesn't come back?" Greasle asked. "What do we do then?"

"I don't know. But we have three days to come up with a plan. Now, quiet—I have to think." The palm tree was too high for him to see into. The tree's trunk offered no branches or footholds. He turned to Greasle. "I'm going to give you a boost. Check and tell me what it looks like."

"Right-o." Greasle scampered off his shoulder and up the tree. She peered into the branches and wrinkled her nose. "Ain't nothing but a bunch of ashes and twigs. Not even a feather left."

"That's what Aunt Phil said would happen. Is it still warm?"

"Yep. Could roast a frankfurter on it. Hey! There's an idea."

"Except we don't have any frankfurters," Nate reminded her. Greasle's face fell, and he almost laughed at how sad she looked. Then he glanced up at the sky. It was nearly fully dark—and the temperature was falling fast.

"Come on," he said. "I need to read up on my duties."

Back inside the tent, Nate lit one of the lanterns they had brought and took *The Book of Beasts* from Aunt Phil's pack. The thick, aged pages crinkled slightly at his touch.

Greasle clambered up to perch on his shoulder. "Are us gremlins in there?"

Nate thumbed past pages on manticores, basilisks, unicorns, griffins, wyverns, and something called a kraken. "Not that I can see."

"Stupid book," Greasle muttered.

He found the page on the phoenix next to a map of Arabia. He read quickly. "Keep the ash in the nest warm, protect from cold and wind, add additional fuel. Got it." He started to close the book, then saw there was a second page about the phoenix.

There are many magical properties attributed to the phoenix:

If a sick or wounded man hears the song of a phoenix, he will be healed.

Phoenix tears, if drunk, will provide eternal life.

A phoenix feather is said to possess many magical properties. Unfortunately, there is no record of what they are.

A pinch of ashes from the fire of a phoenix can cure the gaze of a basilisk, the bite of a manticore, the scratch from a dragon's claw, or any human illness.

Once a phoenix is finished with his nest, he will gather all the ash and twig into an egg. In ancient times he carried the egg to the temple of the sun god. It is considered a most precious offering.

Nate closed the book gently. Interesting, but it wouldn't help him keep the ashes warm. He set the book down and searched the tent until he found the pile of cinnamon twigs. He grabbed a handful, then hurried outside to the palm tree.

How was he to reach the nest? He looked around for something he could stand on, but there was nothing. He ran back into the tent and began dragging Shabiib's saddle outside. The hard wooden frame would make a perfect step stool.

Greasle ran over and hopped up onto the saddle. "Whee!" she said.

"You're not helping." Nate gritted his teeth. The soft sand dragged against the saddle, making it hard to pull.

"Aw, come on. I don't weigh much, and this is the most fun I've had since you knocked me brother off the propeller."

Guilt poked at Nate, so he said nothing and let Greasle enjoy her ride. Finally, they reached the tree and he shooed her off. Holding steady against the trunk of the palm, he stood up on the saddle. He could see a small bed of glowing ash. Nate sighed in relief. It hadn't gone out, which meant he hadn't ruined anything. Not yet, anyway.

"Don't worry," he whispered to the pile of ash. "I won't let the fire go out. I promise." He took a couple of cinnamon twigs from his pocket and fed them into the embers.

As the night breeze picked up, he turned his thoughts to creating a shelter for the nest.

He could fashion a tent of some kind, but if the Bedouin came back, they would see it and perhaps figure out there was a second person. It was too bad the palm fronds didn't grow straight up, like a wall. Then he wouldn't even have to worry about the wind.

That was it! He looked at the other palm trees around the oasis. He could borrow some of their leaves. He hopped down from the saddle, then began dragging it to the next closest tree. Greasle hopped onboard. "Whatcha doin' now?"

"I'm going to make a windbreak." Nate tugged harder on the saddle. "But I need palm leaves for it."

"Why didn't you say so?" Greasle hopped off and scampered up the tree. A second later, her head popped out from behind the leaves. "How many do you want?"

"Uh, five or six ought to do it."

Her tiny hands neatly snapped the leaves from the tree. Nate gathered them into a pile, then dragged the saddle back, Greasle hopping onboard once more. Hot and

sweaty, Nate picked up the first palm frond and climbed up onto the saddle.

After thinking about it, he decided to weave the leaves together, like Miss Lumpton braiding her hair. A sharp wave of homesickness for his own little room flooded him, but he pushed it aside and got to work.

A long time later, he tucked the last palm frond into position. He leaned back to survey his handiwork. It was a bit lopsided and the leaves stuck out at odd angles, but it held. And it would keep the wind out. Even better, it blended in with the existing leaves so that it wouldn't be detected.

Nate glanced up at the sky. Once the sun rose, his work would be done and he could get some sleep. He fed a couple more twigs into the glowing ash and waited for it to grow warm.

As soon as the sun's rays shone down on the nest, Nate dragged the saddle back into the tent. Then he dropped onto his bedroll, every muscle sore and tired, his body screaming for sleep.

Greasle scurried over and sat on his chest. "Do you think they'll notice them tracks in the sand if they come back?"

Nate groaned. "You're right." He forced himself to get

to his feet and went back outside. He found a loose palm frond and used it to erase the tracks he'd made with the saddle. Too tired to even think, he returned to the tent and collapsed face-down onto his bedroll.

He was just drifting off to sleep when he heard voices.

Chapter Twelve

NATE ROLLED TO HIS KNEES. Greasle froze with a date halfway to her mouth.

Nate crawled to the tent flap and peered outside.

A group of Bedouin girls carrying water skins dismounted from their camels. Chatting excitedly in Arabic, they pointed at the tent as they made their way to the water's edge. Nate ducked farther back into the shadows. He held his breath and watched. One girl set her water skin down and went to study the ground at the base of the tree where the phoenix nest was. Nate had left a couple of unused palm leaves on the ground.

Luckily, two of the other girls began scolding her to fill her water skin and she was called away from the tree. Once they'd filled their skins, the girls lugged them back to the camels and strapped them on. Nate's whole body sagged in relief as he watched them ride away.

"That was close," Greasle said.

"Too close." Nate turned from the tent flap. "What if they had decided to look in here? We would have been discovered for sure."

"We could have hidden behind those packs there."

"Yes, but there are two bedrolls. They'd know that Aunt Phil had been lying when she said she'd come alone."

"Ooh. Right you are!"

All thought of sleep forgotten, Nate sprang into action.

"What are you doing?" Greasle asked.

"I'm packing up all of Aunt Phil's things. Then, if they come back and decide to explore the tent, it will look like only one person ever meant to sleep here."

When Nate did finally sleep, it was fitfully. He jerked

awake at every noise, afraid the girls—or worse, the men—
had returned. Finally, near late afternoon he gave up. He
untangled himself from his bedroll, picked up his sketchbook, and drew until nightfall.

The second night passed much as the first, except Nate had
to enlist Greasle's aid in keeping awake. He'd instructed
her to pinch him every time he started to fall asleep. She'd
taken to her duties a little too eagerly, he thought. By the
time morning came, he was black and blue all over.

"Quit complaining. You're still awake, aren't ya?" Greasle pointed out.

He stumbled to the tent, grabbed a breakfast of dried meat and dates, then fell face first onto his bedroll. He felt Greasle's weight on his back as she climbed on top of him. "Can't you find someplace else to sleep?" he asked.

"Oh, all right," she grumbled. "But creatures is supposed to sleep in packs, you know."

Nate didn't know. He had no idea how creatures were supposed to sleep or, indeed, anything about them.

Greasle pinched him.

"Ow! I'm sorry I didn't know you were supposed—"

Greasle clamped one of her tiny hands across his mouth. "Shh! They're coming."

Nate rolled over and crawled back to the tent flap. Four mounted camels approached the oasis. Listening carefully, he could detect the girls' voices.

"Hide!" he whispered.

He and Greasle scrambled over to one of the large saddles along the side of the tent. Nate curled up on the ground behind one and pulled the saddle blanket over himself. Greasle wiggled up next to him.

They held perfectly still as they listened to the girls at the water's edge. The girls' voices rose and fell as they filled their water skins. After what seemed like forever, Nate heard the voices change position. But instead of moving away, they were coming toward the tent!

Alarmed, Nate listened to the voices draw closer and closer. He heard a *whoosh* as the flap door was thrown open. Silence hung in the air, and then the girls began whispering.

Nate's hiding place stank of camel and he tried not to sneeze. He made himself as small as possible and hoped they wouldn't come all the way into the tent.

He heard a rustling sound as a pack was opened. There was more rustling as the girls came into the tent and began rifling through all their things. After an eternity, they seemed to grow tired of their game. With a last flurry of giggles, they left the tent.

Nate went weak with relief. He waited a few more moments to be sure they'd gone, then crawled over to the tent flap. He peered out in time to see one lone girl returning to the oasis. She climbed off her camel, then went to retrieve the water skin she'd left behind.

As she walked past the tree with the phoenix nest, she hesitated. Had she seen the windbreak? Noticed something unusual about the tree? Slowly, she set the water skin down and walked toward the tree. When she was close enough, she raised her hands and gripped the trunk. *She was going to climb it! She would disturb the nest!*

Without pausing to think, Nate was out of the tent in a heartbeat. "Wait! Don't!"

Shocked, the girl froze with her hands on the tree.

Too late, Nate realized he'd just given himself away.

Chapter Thirteen

SLOWLY, THE GIRL STEPPED BACK from the tree and turned to face him. They stared at each other warily.

"Who are you?" the girl asked in halting English.

"Nathaniel Fludd. Who are you?"

"Fadia, daughter of Khalid Jabbaar." She lifted her chin. "This is our oasis. You shouldn't be here."

"I-I have been sent to watch over the phoenix," Nate said.

The girl narrowed her eyes. "The phoenix!" She studied

him a moment, then looked over her shoulder at the tree. "They say that is but a myth."

Nate shook his head. "No. It's real."

Fadia took a step closer. "You have seen it?"

"Yes. It was the most beautiful thing I've ever seen," he said simply.

"If there was a phoenix, it belongs to us."

"I don't think something like a phoenix really belongs to anybody," Nate said.

"Perhaps that is true," she said. "But *you* do not belong *here*. This oasis is ours."

"I just need to stay for another day or two. I promise not to harm anything."

Fadia shook her head. "It is not my place to say yes or no. I have a duty to report you to my tribe. They will decide."

"No! Please don't tell them." Nate couldn't risk getting captured like Aunt Phil. Who'd be left to tend the nest?

"I must. It is my duty to my tribe."

Before Nate could think of something that would persuade her, Greasle crawled up to his shoulder, and glared at the girl. "He's not going to hurt anything, you big dolt."

Fadia recoiled. "A jinni! You command a jinni?"

"No. It's a gremlin. Not a . . . whatever you said."

Some of the fear left Fadia and she grew haughty again. "What is this gremlin?"

Nate looked from Fadia to Greasle, then back again. He whispered out of the side of his mouth to Greasle, "Just go along with what I say." Then, louder: "Actually, it's our name for jinni."

"How do you have the power over a jinni? You are no older than I?"

Nate tried to look powerful. "It's what my family does. Have power over jinni."

Worry creased Fadia's face. "Please do not set it upon my people."

"Will you keep my presence here a secret?"

She stared at Greasle. "I will do as you ask. I will not tell that you are here."

"Will the rest of them return for water tomorrow?" Nate asked.

Fadia nodded. "Yes, it is our daily chore."

"We will hide again, but try to get them to collect their water and leave right away. No exploring like you did today. If you do exactly as I say, I will not let the jinni harm you."

"Oh, brother," Greasle muttered in his ear. "As if I could hurt a big lug like her." Nate reached up and rubbed away the tickle.

"I promise," Fadia said. With one last nervous glance at Greasle, she scurried over to her camel. She mounted the animal, then left the oasis.

With Greasle still on his shoulder, Nate went over to the palm tree. "That was close," he said. It seemed they'd been saying that a lot lately.

Greasle tugged on his ear. "So what's a jinni, then?"

"I'm not sure," Nate said. "I think I read about them in a book once. They're like an elemental spirit. One that can be controlled by sorcerers and told to do bad things."

Greasle snorted. "You ain't no sorcerer."

"Well, I know that. And you know that. But Fadia doesn't. It was the only bargaining tool we had. If she's afraid you're a jinni and will hurt her people, she'll do what I say. So if we run into the Bedouin again, you be sure to look as jinnilike as you can."

"Right-o." Greasle put her fingers into her mouth and drew it wide open, then wiggled her ears.

"Perfect," Nate said.

Chapter Fourteen

AFTER THE CLOSE CALL WITH FADIA, Nate was finally able to get some rest. He curled up in his bedroll and fell asleep before his head hit the sand.

Hours later, he woke up feeling disoriented. Unsure what had awakened him, he sat up, listening for voices. He heard nothing.

The angle of the light told him it was late afternoon. He'd slept most of the day. Maybe he just woke up because he wasn't tired anymore.

Then he heard it. A faint ripping sound. *That* was what had awakened him.

He looked toward the noise and saw the tip of a knife cutting through the wall of the tent. The blade slowly worked its way through the material, making as little noise as possible.

Once the knife disappeared, a thick, hairy hand emerged through the tear. It groped silently about, as if looking for something.

The hand felt its way toward Aunt Phil's pack. After another minute of groping, it landed on the corner of *The Book of Beasts*. Aunt Phil's words echoed in Nate's head: *I would protect the book with my life*. Before thinking it through, Nate sprang forward and grabbed the book with both hands. The intruder's hand gripped tighter, its knuckles growing white.

"Greasle! Help!" Nate yelled, not knowing what else to do.

The gremlin joined him. She gripped the stranger's hand and sank her sharp little teeth into it.

There was a bellow of pain. The hand let go of the book and flung the gremlin off. Greasle did a somersault, came

up on her feet, and hurried over to the tent flap. Nate was close on her heels, the book safely in his hands.

They stumbled outside in time to see a man in black robes running to a waiting camel. Once he'd clambered onto the animal's back, it lurched to its feet and broke into a run. The man's turban was knocked from his head. Nate only had time to note that the intruder had bushy ginger-colored hair before he disappeared over the ridge.

"Who was that, I'd like to know!" Greasle spat. "He tasted right awful, he did."

"I don't know. But I think he was after Aunt Phil's *Book of Beasts*."

"Why would anyone want that stupid ol' thing?"

"I don't know," Nate said. He was tired of that answer. There were so very many things he didn't know. A sick feeling rose up in his stomach. But then Greasle came over and leaned up against him. Her warm presence at his side reminded him that he had done the right thing by her. Even if it had meant disagreeing with Aunt Phil.

A cool breeze stirred. Nate glanced overhead. The sun had set. It was time to tend the nest. Even if he failed at everything else, he could still try to get that right.

He shoved the book into his rucksack, then slung the pack over his shoulders and got to work.

Greasle quickly grew bored watching the nest. She curled up and fell asleep at Nate's feet.

Perched atop the saddle, he leaned against the palm tree and fed a cinnamon twig into the smoldering ash. Was it just his imagination or had the ash taken on a more solid shape? It seemed lumpier to him. If he squinted his eyes, it was almost bird shaped.

"What am I going to do about Aunt Phil?" he asked the small pile of ash. "How can I rescue her when I have no camels, no weapons, nothing?"

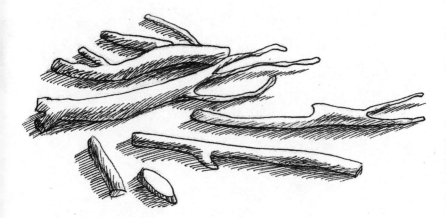

"Who are you talking to?" Greasle asked sleepily from her spot near his feet.

"No one," Nate said, embarrassed to have been caught. "Just thinking out loud."

"Well, stop it." Greasle yawned. "Some of us wants to sleep."

"Sorry," Nate mumbled. He kept his mouth firmly closed while his mind worked furiously to come up with a plan.

Chapter Fifteen

W*HEN THE MORNING OF THE THIRD DAY DAWNED*, Nate still didn't have a plan. The Bedouin period of hospitality would soon be over and Aunt Phil would be tried for trespassing.

Discouraged, he fed the last cinnamon twig into the ash just as the sun rose over the ridge. He turned to watch the gold and pink rays shoot out across the oasis.

There was a crackling sound behind him, drawing Nate's attention back to the nest.

It glowed bright red now and was definitely a lump. As he watched, the lump began to grow. It stretched up and up and began to fill out.

The snowy ash that clung to the shape shifted, fluttering in the morning breeze. Nate blinked. It was no longer ash, but tiny white and gray feathers. The body of the phoenix—for that's what it was—began to glow brightly. Colors spread out from the body to the ash, until all of it was bright orange and red.

Two small black eyes appeared next. The phoenix turned its head and met Nate's gaze. A wondrous feeling shot through him. A feeling that he could do anything in the world, if only he set his mind to it.

The phoenix opened its beak and melodious notes floated into the morning air. If hope and joy had a sound, Nate thought, it would be just like that. At his feet, Greasle sat up to listen.

Without any warning at all, the phoenix raised its wings and rose from the nest. Orange and gold tail feathers unfurled behind it like a glowing shower of sparks.

Nate watched the phoenix's first flight. As it circled the

oasis, it began singing again, the pure, joyous notes filling the air.

Greasle sighed. "That really is the most lovely sound."

The phoenix circled the oasis one last time before coming in closer to Nate. As it drew near, it thrust out its clawed feet. Nate flinched, afraid for a moment that the bird was attacking him.

Instead, it landed on his shoulder, so gentle he barely even felt it. Nate froze, afraid to move and disturb the magnificent creature. It weighed hardly anything, as if it were truly nothing but ash and smoke. It reached out and nibbled gently at Nate's ear with its beak.

"I think it likes you," Greasle said.

Nate felt himself blush with pleasure. "Maybe." He risked turning his head so that he could look into the phoenix's eyes. The bird tilted its head and their gazes met. It was as if the phoenix were looking deep inside him, taking his measure. Nate felt naked, his every secret hope and fear painfully laid bare before the phoenix's knowing gaze.

But as he continued to stare into the phoenix's eyes, Nate noticed something else. His hopes began to grow, filling up

and spreading out until there was hardly any room left over for fear. His exhaustion and discouragement were burned away, like clouds before the sun, leaving only his possibilities behind.

As if satisfied, the phoenix broke eye contact and trilled one final note before launching itself back to the nest. Unable to look away, Nate followed, standing on the saddle to get a closer look.

The phoenix was doing something with all the leftover ash in its nest. As Nate watched, it gathered it into a tidy little egg-shaped pile. As the ash and embers cooled, the egg hardened. The phoenix grabbed it in its claws, then rose up into the air and held the egg out to Nate.

"For me?" Nate asked, unable to believe he was being given such a precious gift.

The phoenix ducked its head, as if nodding, so Nate took the egg. "Thank you," he said, cradling it in his palms. The phoenix let out a burst of song, circled the oasis twice, then disappeared over the eastern horizon.

The egg in Nate's hand was smooth and glossy and still slightly warm. Small clumps of ash clung to it in places. Colors swirled deep inside it. As he stared at the egg in his hand, a plan began to form. Miss Lumpton had been very pleased to receive a Tidy Sum for taking care of him. Maybe the Bedouin would like to receive a gift for taking care of Aunt Phil? Surely a phoenix egg was better than plain old money?

He carefully wrapped the egg in his soft leather helmet, then placed it in his rucksack next to *The Book of Beasts*. With Greasle at his heels, he climbed the eastern ridge. At the top, he shielded his eyes against the rising sun. There. He could see the Bedouin camp in the distance. That was where he had to go.

Chapter Sixteen

NATE SET OUT DOWN THE RIDGE, where the sun had only just risen. Hopefully he'd reach the camp before the girls set out for their midmorning trip to the oasis. He didn't want to be caught out in the open like this. Mounted on camels, it would take them no time to raise the alarm. He preferred to sneak into the camp to be sure Aunt Phil was okay before announcing his presence.

The distance was a lot farther than it looked, and for the first time, he found himself missing Shabiib.

Greasle grew tired halfway there and he had to carry her on his shoulders.

When the group of tents finally came into sight, Nate got down and began to belly crawl the rest of the way.

He reached the camels first. They were all grouped off to the side of the tents. If he used them as cover, it would hide his approach.

Slowly he crawled forward until he was practically under the camels' hooves. Now what?

He peered through the camels' legs toward the tents. Most of the people seemed to be tending small cooking fires as they started their day. No one looked like Aunt Phil, which meant she must be inside one of the tents.

But which one? There were more than a dozen. He

couldn't very well search every tent. And he dared not get any closer to the Bedouin.

"So now what?" Greasle asked, echoing his thoughts.

"Now we find Aunt Phil, I trade the phoenix egg for her, and then we all go home."

"Are you sure she's worth it?" Greasle said. "I mean, that fiery bird gave it to you. Seems like he wanted *you* to have it."

"I know," Nate said. The feeling that he was betraying the phoenix's gift had haunted him all morning. "But it's the only thing I have of value. Now, the sooner you go over there and see where Aunt Phil is, the sooner we can all go home."

"Me?" Greasle squealed.

"Shh! Yes, you. You're so small, they probably won't even see you. And if they do, they'll just think you're a jinni, like Fadia did. They'll leave you alone."

"No, sir. I don't think so. Besides, why should I help her?"

"Well, Aunt Phil let you stay with us."

Greasle snorted.

Nate thought a moment longer. "You want to get back to the plane, don't you? I won't be able to find my way back on my own. We'll need Aunt Phil to help us get there."

Greasle's ears drooped, and Nate could tell he'd won.

"Okay, then," she said.

"And remember," he said. "If they catch you, act like a jinni. It's our best weapon."

Greasle nodded, then leaped forward and disappeared within seconds. Nate held his breath, terrified he would hear a shout from the men signaling they'd spotted her.

But nothing happened. He waited so long that his legs began to cramp. Just when he was worried that something had happened to Greasle, Nate felt something damp and prickly against his leg. He whipped around and found himself staring into the face of a camel. The camel worked his lips a couple of times. *Oh, no,* Nate thought, but before he could roll out of the way, the camel shot a thick wad of stinky spit at him. *Shabiib,* he thought as he wiped the mess away.

"Shoo!" Nate whispered, then turned back around to keep a watch out for Greasle and Aunt Phil.

A group of men emerged from one of the larger tents. They were all talking together importantly. Nate leaned forward, straining to hear their voices.

There was another nudge on his ankle. He jiggled his foot, shaking Shabiib off. "Not now, you stupid cam—" His words were cut off as an iron grip took ahold of his collar and hauled him to his feet.

Chapter Seventeen

NATE DANGLED THREE FEET from the ground. An angry dark gaze met his. "What have we here? A camel thief?"

"No!" Nate cried out, shocked someone would think such a thing. "I've just come for my aunt."

The Bedouin looked from Nate to Shabiib, his expression unreadable. "We will see what our sheik has to say about that." He set Nate's feet on the ground but kept a firm grip on his collar as he marched him toward the largest tent. Everyone stopped to stare. One girl raised her hand to her mouth in surprise. It was Fadia. She quickly looked away.

As he was propelled toward the tent, Nate glanced around frantically, trying to locate Greasle. This would be the perfect time for her to appear and do her jinni routine. But she was nowhere in sight.

The Bedouin threw open the tent flap and shoved Nate inside. He barely managed to keep from stumbling.

Five men looked up and their conversation came to an abrupt halt. Nate blinked, trying to adjust to the dim light.

"What have you brought us, Khalid?" asked an older man wearing a fancier robe than the others. The sheik, presumably.

"Another trespasser. Possibly a camel thief. Possibly a spy. Perhaps our honored guest knows something about it." It was then that Nate saw Aunt Phil seated regally on a floor cushion, watching all of them. "Does he belong to you?" Khalid asked.

"Yes, he does."

"Actually," Nate said, speaking for the first time, "I'm here to offer a trade."

"A trade?"

"Yes." He wiped his sweaty palms on his trousers and

cleared his throat. "In, um, appreciation for your hospitality toward my aunt. I've come to offer a gift for her return."

"I am listening," the sheik said.

His heart beating fast, Nate slipped his hand into his pack and closed it around the smooth, perfect phoenix egg. He dreaded giving it away, but he had nothing else to offer.

"Well? What do you have?" the sheik asked, growing impatient.

Nate pulled the egg out. "I have a rare phoeni—"

Aunt Phil gasped. "Nate! No!"

The sheik stared at it, his face expressionless. "You offer me a rock?"

"No, no. It isn't a rock. This is a phoenix egg! The phoenix gave it to me after it emerged from the ashes."

The sheik's face grew stern. "The phoenix is a creature of myth and belongs to the old tales. Your rock is of no value to me. Now, go sit with your aunt while we decide what must be done about you."

Nate couldn't believe his ears—couldn't they tell this was no ordinary rock? He opened his mouth to argue, but Khalid caught his eye. "Go," he said. "Arguing will do you no good."

With the bitter taste of failure in his mouth, Nate went to sit beside Aunt Phil.

"May I see it?" Aunt Phil asked, her eyes bright with excitement.

"Sure." Nate pulled the lustrous egg out and handed it to her. At least she understood how special it was.

"Extraordinary," she murmured, turning it over in her hands. She looked up at Nate, her eyes shining. "Excellent work."

"Well, thanks. But fat lot of good it does us."

"Don't worry." She handed the egg back to him. "We'll think of some—"

There was a mad howl, and then something crashed into Nate's shoulder.

Greasle! he thought as the gremlin raced past him on all fours. Nate hoped these men were as afraid of jinn as Fadia had been.

Chapter Eighteen

GREASLE BARELY SPARED NATE A GLANCE as she ran by him, headed straight for the door.

"What was that?" the sheik asked.

"A jinni?" Nate offered hopefully. The men got to their feet and followed the gremlin out of the tent. Nate and Aunt Phil hurried after them.

"What is your gremlin up to now?" Aunt Phil whispered.

"Don't worry. It's all part of our plan." But Greasle wasn't acting the least bit jinnilike. In fact, she was acting more like a hound on the scent of a tasty bone. She was still on all fours, sniffing at the ground. After a moment, she began digging furiously.

Warily, the Bedouin gathered round, pointing and whispering. Nate pushed to the front of the crowd.

Greasle was rolling in a small trickle of thick, dark liquid. She paused to slurp up a big gulp, then writhed with happiness. At Nate's approach, she looked up and grinned. "Much better than nasty dates," she said gleefully.

Nate knelt and dipped his fingers into the puddle. He sniffed, then rubbed them together. He looked up at Aunt Phil. "It's just like that stuff you had in the barrel for your airplane," he said.

Aunt Phil knelt and tested the puddle herself. "You're right, Nate. It is oil."

Nate thought a moment. "You said it was valuable. Will they trade it for our freedom?"

Aunt Phil's eyes widened in surprise. "They just might." She raised her voice and called out to the sheik, "Our gremlin—er, jinni—has given you a gift of great value. She has discovered oil."

"Oil?" the sheik repeated. "What is this oil? It is not water and we cannot drink it. Of what value can it be?"

Aunt Phil scooped up a handful of the oozing black liquid and let it dribble from her fingers. "This is what will power the future," she said. "Airplanes, motorcars, trucks, tanks—all need this substance in order to run. Men will pay much for it."

The sheik narrowed his eyes. "You mean the machines of war. Like the Turks and British used to fight."

Aunt Phil looked sad for a moment. "Yes. Your first taste of our technology was in war. But there are many other uses for such machines. Oil may not have value for the Bedouin, but others will pay dearly for it. It will bring you much in trade."

The sheik studied Greasle, who now lay in an oily stupor, her little belly bulging. Then he looked back at Nate. "Very well. We will take this in trade for your aunt. But come," he said to Aunt Phil. "Tell me more of this oil and fuel and technology. I want to understand your view of the future. Then we will return your camels to you and see you on your way."

Aunt Phil looked over her shoulder at Nate. "Brilliant!" she said.

Hours later, Nate and Aunt Phil were escorted to the oasis. They rode behind two Bedouin, leading their own camels by ropes.

Once they had bid goodbye to the Bedouin, Aunt Phil looked toward the palm tree, her face forlorn. "I can't believe I missed the phoenix. Was it wonderful?" she asked.

Nate stared at the tree, remembering. "It was better than wonderful."

After another moment, Aunt Phil sighed and draped her arm across Nate's shoulders. It felt odd—heavy, but nice, too. "Well, there's no doubt about it. You're an official Fludd now. The only one of us to see a phoenix rebirth since 1428."

Nate stood up a little taller and tried to look official.

"You'll have to tell me every detail of what happened so I can record it in *The Book of Beasts*."

The Book of Beasts! Nate had almost forgotten. "Aunt Phil, when you were at the Bedouin camp, did you see a man with red hair? Sort of the same color as yours? He was short and round and wore black robes."

"No," Aunt Phil said, suddenly alert. "Why?"

Nate told her of the attempt to steal *The Book of Beasts*. When he was done, she began to pace. "What? What's wrong?" he asked.

"Describe him to me again," she said.

Nate did. When he was done, he asked, "Do you have any idea who it might have been?"

Aunt Phil stopped pacing and sighed. "I have my suspicions. There are very few who even know the book exists. If I am right, it's very bad news indeed." Her face cleared. "But excellent work in keeping it safe, Nate."

"Greasle helped," he pointed out.

Aunt Phil glanced at the sleeping gremlin. "I must say, she's proven far more useful than I ever imagined."

As Aunt Phil turned away, Greasle opened one eye and winked at Nate. He winked back.

"Now," Aunt Phil said, "let's get on back to the plane. We've loads to do and little time to do it." She lifted her saddle, grunting with the effort, and headed toward her camel.

Nate followed behind. "Really?" Nate asked. "What's next?"

"Well, not only do we need to put out some inquiries about this would-be thief of yours, but I want to locate your Miss Lumpton. I have a few questions I'd like to ask her."

That would be interesting, Nate thought. He could hardly imagine the two of them in the same room.

"And as if that weren't enough," she continued, "we need to make a quick trip to visit the wyverns. It's time for the wyvern hatchlings to begin flying soon, and I don't want the chickens and goats to begin disappearing at an alarming rate. Here." She reached into her pocket and tossed something at Nate.

Startled, Nate managed to catch it. He turned it round and round in his hands. It was a compass, just like hers. The engraved dodo on the cover looked so real, Nate half expected him to talk.

"The Fludd family compass," Aunt Phil explained. "It's high time your formal training began. We've loads of catching up to do."

Nate slipped the compass into his pocket. He couldn't wait to get back to Aunt Phil's house and show that stuffy old dodo just how wrong he'd been.

The End

NATHANIEL FLUDD'S GUIDE TO PEOPLE, PLACES, AND THINGS

airship *Italia*: a semirigid airship, or dirigible, designed by Umberto Nobile that crashed in the Arctic Circle on May 23, 1928

Bedouin: nomadic tribes that live in the deserts of the Middle East

Budapest: the capital of Hungary, one of the early stops on the airmail routes from England

cardinal points: the four primary directions on a compass (north, south, east, and west)

cartographer: a mapmaker

compass: a navigational instrument that indicates direction with its magnetic needle always pointing north

compass rose: a small drawing on a map that shows the orientation of the map

dodo bird: a large, flightless bird thought extinct since the mid-seventeenth century

the Great War: the global war (now often called World War I) that took place from 1914 to 1918. It was one of the largest wars in history and involved many of the world's major powers.

gremlin: a small, greasy creature first discovered by Great War pilots when it fouled their engines and mechanical workings

Mungo Fludd: the first Fludd of record. In 1422, he set out to retrace the steps of Marco Polo so that he could map the world. He ended up traveling the globe for seventeen years (often called the Great Wandering). He was the first European to see the birth of a phoenix in 1428.

oasis: a spring or water source found in a desert

oil: a thick, heavy substance for motor engines and other industrial uses

ordinal points: the four compound directions on a compass (northeast, southeast, northwest, and southwest)

phoenix: a mythical bird that is able to regenerate itself every five hundred years and is said to possess many magical properties

Sopwith Platypus: a lesser-known biplane created during the Great War by the Sopwith Aviation Company as part of the Sopwith Zoo that is able to land on both water and land

Spitsbergen: an island in the Arctic Circle and the last known location of Horatio and Adele Fludd

Tidy Sum: a large amount of money

Turks: members of the Turkish state also known as the Ottoman Empire prior to the Great War